CRYPTS, TOMBS, AND SECRET ROOMS

WESTMINSTER ABBEY

BY ENZO GEORGE

Gareth Stevens
PUBLISHING

Please visit our website, www.garethstevens.com. For a free color catalog of all our high-quality books, call toll-free 1-800-542-2595 or fax 1-877-542-2596.

Cataloging-in-Publication Data
Names: George, Enzo.
Title: Westminster Abbey / Enzo George.
Description: New York : Gareth Stevens Publishing, 2018. | Series: Crypts, tombs, and secret rooms | Includes index.
Identifiers: ISBN 9781538206645 (pbk.) | ISBN 9781538206584 (library bound) | ISBN 9781538206461 (6 pack)
Subjects: LCSH: Funeral rites and ceremonies--England. | Nobility--Great Britain. | Westminster Abbey.
Classification: LCC DA687.W5 G47 2018 | DDC 942.1'32--dc23

Published in 2018 by
Gareth Stevens Publishing
111 East 14th Street, Suite 349
New York, NY 10003

For Brown Bear Books Ltd:
Managing Editor: Tim Cooke
Designer: Lynne Lennon
Editorial Director: Lindsey Lowe
Children's Publisher: Anne O'Daly
Design Manager: Keith Davis
Picture Manager: Sophie Mortimer

Picture credits:
Cover: suraark
Interior: Alamy: Mirrorpix 35; **Canterbury Cathedral:** 20; **Dean and Chapter of Westminster Abbey:** 5, 12, 17, 21, 23, 24, 25, 28, 29, 36, 39, 43; **Dreamstime:** Ivan Kravtsov 19, Marina Ivanova 27, Zefart 37; **Getty Images:** Dan Kitwood: 34; **Kenneth Wilson:** 32, 38; **Musee du Loufre:** 31; **National Portrait Gallery:** 26; **Petworth House:** 18; **Robert Hunt Library:** 9, 10, 14, 15, 40; **Shutterstock:** Christoph Lischetzki 6, Claudio Divizia 7, Pack-shot 11, Francisco Javier Gil 13, kiev.victor 16, Krasowit 22, Anton Ivanov 30, 33, r.nagy 41, Dutourdumonde Photography 42; **TopFoto:** Woodmansterne 8.

All other images Brown Bear Books

Printed in the United States of America
CPSIA compliance information: Batch CS17GS: For further information contact Gareth Stevens, New York, New York at 1-800-542-2595.

CONTENTS

WORDS IN THE GLOSSARY APPEAR IN **BOLD** TYPE THE FIRST TIME THEY ARE USED IN THE TEXT.

THE TOMBS OF MONARCHS

Westminster Abbey in London is one of the most famous churches in the world. It is also the final resting place of many of Great Britain's kings and queens. For more than 1,000 years, since the 1000s, Westminster Abbey has been a royal church at the heart of British life. Building of the current church began in 1245, but a religious building has stood on the site since at least 960, and possibly earlier.

Today, Westminster Abbey plays a central role in British **ceremonial** life as the setting for many royal occasions, such as weddings and funerals. More than 3,000 people are buried or have **memorials** in Westminster Abbey. These memorials **commemorate** many leading figures from British history.

Before the current church was built, King Edward the Confessor built a church on the site. His tomb now stands near the High Altar.

STONES OF THE PAST

Westminster Abbey stands on the north bank of the Thames River on a site that 1,000 years ago was a marshy island called Thorney Island. Henry III (reigned 1216–1272) began building the present church on the site of an earlier church, but it was more than 250 years before it was finally completed.

The church is built in the shape of a cross with a long nave and two short wings, called transepts.

The cloister was a covered walkway where monks could walk and study in a quiet environment.

THE ABBEY BUILDINGS

Sometime around 960, the Bishop of London, St. Dunstan of Canterbury, sent a group of monks to Thorney Island on the Thames River to found a **Benedictine** monastery. King Edgar (reigned 959–975) gave the monks land, but it was not until 100 years later, during the reign of King Edward (1042–1066), that the monastery expanded. The monks built a church next to the monastery where local people worshiped. Arranged around a large cloister were various buildings for the monks, including a refectory where they ate, a dormitory where they slept, and the chapter house where they met. The monastery was home to between 30 and 60 monks.

THORNEY ISLAND

THORNEY ISLAND WAS A SMALL, MARSHY PATCH OF LAND FORMED WHERE THE TYBURN RIVER, WHICH FLOWED THROUGH NORTH LONDON, MET THE THAMES. IN MEDIEVAL TIMES, MONKS CLEARED THE THORNY BRAMBLES THAT GAVE THE ISLAND ITS NAME AND TURNED IT INTO GREEN FIELDS. KING EDWARD'S DECISION TO BUILD HIS CHURCH THERE PUT THE ISLAND AT THE CENTER OF ENGLISH LIFE. TODAY, THE ISLAND HAS BECOME PART OF THE NORTH BANK OF THE THAMES.

This illustration shows the abbey and other buildings on Thorney Island in the late Middle Ages. As the channel between the riverbank and the island was filled in, the island became part of the mainland.

A small town grew up outside the monastery walls. The church and the town became known as Westminster, because the church was the **minster** west of the City of London, which had its own minster (St. Paul's Cathedral).

EDWARD THE CONFESSOR

Edward began to replace the monks' church with a new abbey. He moved his palace to Westminster from Winchester to be near the church. Westminster Palace, opposite the abbey, was the main residence for the English king throughout the Middle Ages. Edward was very sick by the time the church was **consecrated** on December 28, 1065, and died days later on January 5, 1066.

Edward had a reputation for being a devoted Christian. That is why he was known as Edward the Confessor.

EDWARD'S ABBEY

THE ABBEY IN WESTMINSTER TODAY IS NOT THE ABBEY EDWARD BUILT. EDWARD'S CHURCH WAS BUILT IN THE **ROMANESQUE** STYLE, WHICH FEATURED SEMICIRCULAR ARCHES. IT WAS DEMOLISHED IN 1245. THE ORIGINAL ABBEY WAS BASED ON JUMIÈGES, A BENEDICTINE ABBEY IN NORMANDY, FRANCE. EXPERTS KNOW A LITTLE ABOUT EDWARD'S CHURCH BECAUSE AN IMAGE OF THE ABBEY APPEARS ON THE BAYEUX **TAPESTRY**, WHICH RECORDS THE NORMAN CONQUEST OF ENGLAND IN 1066. THERE ARE ALSO SOME SURVIVING FOUNDATIONS BENEATH THE PRESENT ABBEY.

The Romanesque church was embroidered in the Bayeux Tapestry, the only surviving record of how the original structure looked.

The original abbey was based on the design of Jumièges in Normandy, which now stands without a roof.

Edward had a reputation for good works. After his death, stories began that he had performed miracles. In 1161, the Catholic Church declared Edward a saint and renamed him as "the **Confessor**." Two years later, his body was moved to a **shrine** in front of the **High Altar** in the abbey.

CENTER OF THE COUNTRY

Edward's decision to move his capital made Westminster the most important place in the kingdom. It also ensured that Westminster Abbey would be the most important church in England. After 1350, the House of Commons began to meet in the Chapter House in Westminster Abbey to discuss government business. This was the site of Britain's first **parliament**. The modern Houses of Parliament now stand close to the site.

BUILDING THE MONUMENT

The abbey at Westminster today was built over a period of 250 years to replace the original abbey built by Edward the Confessor. In 1216, Henry III became king of England at the age of just nine. Four years later, Abbot William Humez built a Lady Chapel next to the old abbey to honor the Virgin Mary. The young king was an admirer of Edward the Confessor, and took a great interest in the building. He decided to take on the project, paying for construction and supplying **masons** and craftsmen to do the work.

The king decided to build a church on the site of the existing abbey in the fashionable **Gothic** style. Henry wanted the church to be a magnificent burial place for Edward the Confessor.

A new Lady Chapel at the eastern end of the abbey was built by King Henry VII, who was buried there after his death in 1509.

The rebuilt cathedral at Reims in France may have influenced the design of the new abbey.

Work began on the new abbey in 1245. The master mason was Henry de Reyns, who oversaw the project for the next eight years. He introduced the High Gothic style of architecture to England from France, where the cathedral at Reims had been rebuilt in the style in 1211.

There was little room for the new church. The site was quite small. To the east of the existing abbey was the new Lady Chapel and to the south were the cloisters and other buildings.

To make room, the eastern part of the old church was demolished and replaced with a new eastern wing, the **transepts** — the wings that stick out from the main church at right angles — and the Chapter House.

In June 1253, Master Henry stopped work on the abbey and his name disappeared from all records. A series of other master masons carried on the building work. As the masons worked on construction, craftsmen inside carved stone, made stained-glass windows, and painted decorations.

A LASTING SHRINE

On October 13, 1269, the body of St. Edward the Confessor was laid to rest in its new shrine near the High Altar. Henry III helped to carry Edward's remains into the abbey.

This medieval illustration shows sick people being miraculously cured at the tomb of Edward the Confessor.

A medieval mason builds a wall. Masons traveled around for work, moving on when a project was over.

HENRY DE REYNS

HISTORIANS KNOW VERY LITTLE ABOUT HENRY DE REYNS, THE MASTER MASON RESPONSIBLE FOR THE DESIGN OF WESTMINSTER ABBEY. HE IS ALSO RECORDED AS HAVING WORKED ON WINDSOR CASTLE AND THE TOWER OF LONDON. EXPERTS DO NOT KNOW WHETHER HE WAS ENGLISH OR FRENCH, ALTHOUGH SOME THINK THAT "DE REYNS" MEANT THAT HE WAS FROM THE FRENCH TOWN OF REIMS. THAT WOULD EXPLAIN WHY HE KNEW SO MUCH ABOUT ITS GOTHIC CATHEDRAL.

Three years after Edward the Confessor was reburied, Henry III died. He was buried inside the abbey. Following Henry's death, construction stopped for the next 100 years.

Work started again on the abbey in 1376, this time paid for by Abbot Nicholas Litlyngton with money left by his **predecessor**, Simon Langham. Litlyngton decided that construction should continue and that it should follow King Henry III's original design.

Exterior supports called flying buttresses carry the weight of the roof, preventing the walls from bending outward.

This is the view from between the transepts and the nave, looking up at the Lantern Tower.

The decision to stick to the original plans meant that the style of the abbey remained the same. After Litlyngton, work was continued by Kings Richard II (reigned 1377–1399) and Henry V (1413–1422).

THE END IS IN SIGHT

Work slowed down toward the end of the 1400s. The construction of the abbey had taken so long that it was already looking old fashioned. It looked like a medieval Gothic church when around London new buildings were being designed in the new **Tudor** style, with red brickwork and low arches.

Henry VIII started the Church of England after the pope refused to let him divorce Catherine of Aragon. Henry was eager to marry a wife who would produce a male heir.

By 1509, the main body of the abbey was finally finished. Henry VII (reigned 1485–1509), the first of the Tudor monarchs, ordered the building of the magnificent Lady Chapel for his burial place. Its ceiling had spectacular **fan vaulting**. The chapel was consecrated in 1516.

AN UPHEAVAL

Within only 25 years, the abbey underwent one of the greatest upheavals in its history. Henry VII's son, Henry VIII (reigned (1509–1547), fell out with the Catholic Church when the Pope refused to allow Henry to divorce his wife, Catherine of Aragon. Henry wanted to marry Anne Boleyn. He decided to break with Rome and set up the Church of England, with himself at its head. He closed or destroyed all monasteries and churches in England, including Westminster Abbey. On January 16, 1540, Abbot Boston signed over Westminster Abbey to the king.

CLOSING THE MONASTERIES

DURING THE MIDDLE AGES, THE CATHOLIC CHURCH HAD GROWN VERY RICH IN ENGLAND. THE ABBOTS WHO RAN THE GREAT ABBEYS WERE SOME OF THE RICHEST MEN IN ENGLAND. INSTEAD OF FOLLOWING THEIR VOW OF POVERTY, MANY MONKS LIVED IN GREAT LUXURY. HENRY VIII DECIDED TO BREAK FROM THE CATHOLIC CHURCH AND CREATE HIS OWN PROTESTANT CHURCH. WHEN HE DISSOLVED, OR CLOSED, ALL THE MONASTERIES BETWEEN 1536 AND 1541, HENRY VIII SEIZED THEIR WEALTH FOR THE ENGLISH CROWN, WHICH BECAME HUGELY WEALTHY AS A RESULT.

Whitby Abbey in Yorkshire is one of many ruined religious buildings left in England after the destruction of the monasteries.

SECRETS OF THE PAST

The history of Westminster Abbey is well documented, but there are still some questions that puzzle historians. One question is why the first monks chose to build a church on a marshy island that was full of thorny bramble bushes.

There are a number of stories that might explain their choice. One is about Sebert, the king of the East Saxons who ruled London in the late 500s and early 600s. Sebert was a **pagan** but was converted to Christianity by a **missionary** named Mellitus.

This portrait in stained glass shows St. Mellitus holding a model of Canterbury Cathedral, where he preached in the 600s.

Henry VII was buried in a joint tomb with his wife, Elizabeth of York. His rule was the beginning of the Tudor dynasty.

Mellitus had been sent to England by Pope Gregory in 601 to try to convert the English to Christianity. He built a church on what is now the site of St. Paul's Cathedral in London. Sebert made Mellitus the first bishop of London in 604, and ordered a new church to be built on Thorney Island.

Another account claims that St. Peter appeared to fishermen on the Thames River and told them to build the church on the island. It is said that, in return, St. Peter made sure that the river was always full of fish.

SALMON AT THE ABBEY

THE THAMES RIVER IN CENTRAL LONDON USED TO BE FULL OF FISH INCLUDING SALMON. FOR CENTURIES, THAMES FISHERMEN HAVE REGULARLY GIVEN GIFTS OF SALMON TO THE ABBEY EVERY JUNE 29, WHICH IS ST. PETER'S DAY. THE GIFT THANKS THE SAINT FOR FILLING THE RIVER WITH FISH, AS THE OLD STORY EXPLAINS. THE FISHMONGERS' COMPANY, ONE OF THE TRADE GUILDS OF THE CITY OF LONDON, STILL PRESENTS A SALMON TO WESTMINSTER ABBEY EVERY YEAR.

Pollution caused salmon to disappear from the Thames in London from 1833 until the early 2000s.

St. Peter is also supposed to have appeared to Mellitus on the day that Sebert's church was to be dedicated. It was said that St. Peter miraculously conducted the first service himself.

THE TOMBS OF THE ABBEY

There are tombs throughout Westminster Abbey. The church is home to more than 600 monuments and wall tablets, which makes Westminster Abbey the most important site of **monumental** sculpture in Great Britain. After Henry III reburied Edward the Confessor in a much grander tomb, the abbey became the final resting place for many kings and queens. It also became the resting place for many more people who were noteworthy but not royal. This is a tradition that has continued throughout the years, but its origins are uncertain. It seems to have begun in the 1500s.

The highly ornamented tomb of Elizabeth I lies in the Lady Chapel built by her grandfather, Henry VII.

This collection of memorial stones is part of Poets' Corner. Today, new names are added on panes of a stained glass window.

POETS' CORNER

In 1556, one of England's greatest poets, Geoffrey Chaucer, was laid to rest in a magnificent tomb in part of the south transept of the abbey. Chaucer, who is most famous for writing *The Canterbury Tales*, had actually died in 1400. He was reburied in the abbey not because he was a poet but because he had been an official at the Palace of Westminster. In 1599 another poet, Edmund Spenser, was buried next to Chaucer. Spenser was famous for a long poem in praise of Queen Elizabeth I, *The Faerie Queene*. This began the tradition of Poets' Corner. Since the first two poets' tombs, hundreds more writers, and playwrights have been honored in Poets' Corner.

It is not only writers who have tombs or memorial stones in Poets' Corner—actors and ballet dancers are also honored. Anyone who has made a cultural contribution to British life can be remembered there. The poet T.S. Eliot (1888–1965) was American, but became a British citizen and lived most of his life in England. He has a memorial stone in Poets' Corner.

OTHER SECRETS?

When the playwright William Shakespeare died in 1616, he was buried in his hometown of Stratford-upon-Avon. He was only given a memorial statue in the abbey in 1741. The poet Lord Byron died in 1824. He had to wait until 1969 for a **plaque** in the abbey. Charles Dickens was one of the most popular novelists of the 1800s. When he died in 1870, he did not want a large funeral. Dickens was buried in the abbey very early in the morning on June 14 so that few people would attend.

William Shakespeare's memorial statue was added to Poets' Corner in 1741.

A ROYAL PECULIAR

WESTMINSTER ABBEY ENJOYS AN UNUSUAL STATUS AS A CHURCH. ON MAY 21, 1560, QUEEN ELIZABETH I REFOUNDED THE ABBEY FOLLOWING HER FATHER'S DESTRUCTION OF THE MONASTERIES AND THE DECISION BY HER HALF SISTER, QUEEN MARY, TO BRING BACK CATHOLICISM AS THE STATE RELIGION. ELIZABETH RESTORED THE PROTESTANT FAITH AND MADE WESTMINSTER ABBEY A **COLLEGIATE** CHURCH OR "ROYAL PECULIAR." THIS MEANT THAT THE CHURCH WAS NOT UNDER THE CONTROL OF THE HEAD OF THE PROTESTANT CHURCH, THE ARCHBISHOP OF CANTERBURY. INSTEAD IT WAS UNDER THE DIRECT CONTROL OF THE ENGLISH MONARCH.

Elizabeth I restored Protestantism to England but was tolerant about allowing Catholics to continue to practice their faith.

This photograph shows the Lady Chapel, which is home to many memorials, including those of kings and queens.

When the novelist Thomas Hardy died in 1928, he wanted to be buried with his wife in Dorset, where he lived. Hardy's supporters wanted him buried in Poets' Corner. In the end, Hardy's heart was buried with his first wife in Dorset and his ashes were buried in the abbey.

MORE BURIALS

A similar story relates to the famous missionary and explorer David Livingstone. Livingstone died in Africa in 1873. His heart was buried there, but his body was carried to the coast and shipped to Britain. Livingstone was buried in Westminster Abbey on April 18, 1874.

Also buried in the abbey are scientists such as Isaac Newton and Charles Darwin, composers including Ralph Vaughan Williams, and eight British prime ministers.

INVESTIGATING THE PAST

A church has stood on the site of Westminster Abbey for more than a thousand years. Traces of the earlier churches survive today. They provide fascinating clues about the original building and the story of its creation.

The Pyx Chamber takes its name from the Greek word for boxwood, the material from which the money chest in the chamber was made.

The Cosmati Pavement in front of the High Altar is a detailed mosaic created in the 1200s.

The foundations of Edward's original church have been located beneath the **nave** and **apse** of the current abbey, but they have been built over and are not visible. All that remains of Edward's church are the Pyx Chamber and the **undercroft** in the cloisters. They are the oldest surviving buildings at Westminster, and date from between 1065 and 1090.

PYX CHAMBER

The Pyx Chamber is an underground room that takes its name from the "pyx," or box kept there. The box held pieces of gold and silver that set the standard for how much gold and silver English coins had to contain. The gold and silver were weighed against coins to test them each year.

The Pyx chamber still has its original stone altar and tiled floor. The presence of the stone altar suggests that the room was used as a chapel sometime before the 1300s, when it became the monastery's treasury.

The undercroft in the cloisters was an underground storage room, like a cellar. The Benedictine monks may have also used it as a meeting place.

THE CHAPTER HOUSE

The Chapter House at Westminster Abbey was built in the 1250s in an **octagonal** shape around a central pillar. It has a tiled floor and a fan-vaulted ceiling. Around the edge of the room are stone benches where the monks sat. The Chapter House is an important place in history. It was the place where Parliament met in the 1300s.

The Chapter House was originally built as a place for the monks to meet. It was later home to early parliaments.

THE PRINCES IN THE TOWER

WESTMINSTER ABBEY IS THE FINAL RESTING PLACE OF THE BROTHERS EDWARD V AND RICHARD, DUKE OF YORK. THEY WERE THE SONS OF EDWARD IV, AND WHEN HE DIED IN 1483, EDWARD V BECAME KING AT AGE 12 (RICHARD WAS 9 YEARS OF AGE). THEIR UNCLE, RICHARD, WAS MADE THEIR GUARDIAN. BUT HE IMPRISONED THEM IN THE TOWER OF LONDON, FROM WHERE THEY DISAPPEARED. EXPERTS BELIEVE THAT RICHARD MURDERED THEM TO MAKE HIMSELF KING RICHARD III. IN 1674, WORKMEN FOUND WHAT WERE THOUGHT TO BE THE PRINCES' REMAINS AT THE TOWER. THEY WERE REBURIED IN WESTMINSTER ABBEY.

The fate of the two young brothers is not known, but it is thought that they were murdered by their uncle.

Within the Chapter House is a door that dates from the mid-1000s, known as the "oldest door in Britain." Experts think it was built for Edward's abbey, so it reveals information about Anglo-Saxon carpentry. What remains of the door is made from five vertical oak planks held together with horizontal **battens** covered in animal hide.

A GRUESOME DISCOVERY

In 2015, workers at the abbey began to demolish a toilet block that had been built in the 1950s outside the South Transept. Beneath Victorian drainage pipes, the workers uncovered the skeletons of up to 50 people. Archaeologists examined the bones and learned that they dated from the 1000s and 1100s. They figured out that the bodies must originally have been buried on a small site just outside Edward's original church.

The door in the Chapter House seems to have been cut down from an original that was larger.

THE SCHOOL IN THE ABBEY

WITHIN THE AREA OF WESTMINSTER ABBEY IS ONE OF THE OLDEST SCHOOLS IN GREAT BRITAIN, WESTMINSTER SCHOOL. THE SCHOOL IS THOUGHT BY SOME TO DATE BACK TO BEFORE THE 1100S. SOME HISTORIANS THINK THAT SCHOLARS ATTENDED THE SCHOOL FROM THE EARLIEST DAYS OF THE ABBEY TO WHICH IT WAS ATTACHED, BUT THE STUDENTS MIGHT HAVE BEEN ADULTS. BOYS HAVE BEEN EDUCATED AT THE SCHOOL SINCE 1179. COLLEGE HALL, WHERE THE STUDENTS EAT, IS THE OLDEST CONTINUOUSLY USED DINING HALL IN GREAT BRITAIN.

The ceiling of the octagonal Chapter House is constructed from a series of fan-shaped vaults.

The skeletons at the abbey probably belong to monks who once lived there.

Some of the remains found in 2015 probably belonged to senior **clergy**. The clergy were buried outside the church because only the royal family could be buried inside. Experts believe that, when Henry III was building the present abbey, medieval workers disturbed the graveyard. The workers stacked the bones in a pile, although they left some bodies in their original graves, which were lined with chalk slabs. Such graves were used by the Anglo-Saxons and the Normans who arrived in England in 1066.

There was also a child buried in a wooden coffin and a man buried in a coffin made from expensive stone. The child was too young to be part of the monastery. Historians think the fact that the child was buried in a coffin suggests he or she belonged to a noble family.

WAR DAMAGE

During World War II (1939–1945), the Germans bombed London in a series of nighttime raids known as the Blitz, which lasted from September 7, 1940, until May 21, 1941. On the night of May 10/11, 1941, firebombs hit Westminster Abbey. Flames up to 40 feet (12 m) high burned the abbey. They melted lead on the roof, which splattered over the pulpit and choir stalls. After the war ended in 1945, the abbey was restored. The damage could have been much worse, but fortunately all the movable valuables had been removed from the abbey before the bombing started.

The abbey was damaged by German bombs during the Blitz, but church services were still held there throughout the war.

THE MONUMENT TODAY

Westminster Abbey continues to be at the heart of British life. As well as being a place of worship, it is also a busy tourist destination and a showpiece for the royal family.

Churchgoers, clergy, and choirboys attend a mass in the Lady Chapel.

Westminster Abbey is one of the major tourist sites in London.

The abbey has been a royal church for almost 1,000 years. The shrine of its founder, Edward the Confessor, still lies at the heart of the church. But the abbey is also a working church that welcomes anyone to worship.

There are several services a day, and **saints' days** and days of remembrance are also marked. The abbey even has its own Twitter account.

A TOURIST DESTINATION

Every year, more than one million people visit Westminster Abbey to see attractions such as the Tomb of the Unknown Warrior and the Coronation Chair, which was made for King Edward I (reigned 1272–1307) to house the Stone of Scone, which he brought from Scotland to England in 1296. Millions more people across the world have seen the abbey on live broadcasts of royal events, such as the wedding of the Duke and Duchess of Cambridge in 2011.

The Stone of Scone was kept under the Coronation Chair before it was returned to Scotland in 1996.

THE STONE OF SCONE

THE STONE OF SCONE IS AN OBLONG BLOCK OF PALE YELLOW SANDSTONE. IT WAS ORIGINALLY USED DURING THE CORONATION OF KINGS IN SCOTLAND, WHERE IT WAS KNOWN AS THE "STONE OF DESTINY." EDWARD I BROUGHT IT TO ENGLAND IN 1296 AFTER DEFEATING THE SCOTS IN BATTLE. IT WAS PLACED UNDER THE CORONATION CHAIR AND WAS KNOWN AS THE CORONATION STONE. THE SCOTS HAVE ALWAYS WANTED THE STONE BACK. IN 1950, FOUR SCOTTISH STUDENTS STOLE THE STONE FROM WESTMINSTER ABBEY, BREAKING IT IN THE PROCESS. IT WAS RECOVERED, REPAIRED AND RETURNED TO THE ABBEY. ON NOVEMBER 30, 1996 (ST. ANDREW'S DAY, THE PATRON SAINT OF SCOTLAND), THE STONE WAS FINALLY RETURNED TO EDINBURGH CASTLE.

Tourism plays a vital role in raising money to pay for the upkeep of the abbey, but because Westminster Abbey is primarily a place of worship tourists are not allowed to visit on a Sunday. However, all are welcome to attend services.

THE TOMB OF THE UNKNOWN WARRIOR

Set in the stone floor at the west end of the nave is a black Belgian marble gravestone. An inscription in brass letters identifies the tomb as belonging to "A British Warrior Unknown By Name Or Rank." It is common for heads of state who visit Britain to go to Westminster Abbey to lay a wreath at the tomb.

The idea for the tomb came sometime around the end of World War I. Some graves in France were marked as "An Unknown British Soldier," because many dead soldiers could not be identified.

The Tomb of the Unknown Warrior was intended to be a place to be visited by those whose relatives did not come back from World War I.

It was decided that a permanent tomb to the fallen of World War I would serve as a memorial that those who had lost loved ones in the war, but had no grave to visit, could go to. A body was brought from the battlefields of France and buried on November 11, 1920 (**Remembrance Day** and the anniversary of the end of World War I), in the presence of the royal family. The grave was filled with soil from France.

CORONATIONS

Since the coronation of William the Conqueror in 1066, British monarchs have been crowned in the abbey. The head of the Church of England, the Archbishop of Canterbury, performs the ceremony.

Elizabeth II (bottom, center) leaves the abbey having been crowned as queen on June 2, 1953.

The current St. Paul's Cathedral is the fifth version of the church to have stood on the site.

ST. PAUL'S CATHEDRAL

WESTMINSTER ABBEY WAS NAMED TO DISTINGUISH IT FROM THE OTHER MAJOR CHRISTIAN CHURCH IN LONDON. ST. PAUL'S CATHEDRAL WAS OLDER AND HAD BEEN BUILT IN 604 IN THE CITY OF LONDON, TO THE EAST. THE ABBEY WAS THEREFORE NAMED "WEST MINSTER." THE ORIGINAL CATHEDRAL AT ST. PAUL'S BURNED DOWN. ITS REPLACEMENT WAS LATER DESTROYED, AS WELL. A THIRD CATHEDRAL WAS BUILT, BUT BURNED DOWN YET AGAIN IN 1087. ONCE AGAIN, THE CATHEDRAL WAS REPLACED AND THIS TIME DESTROYED IN THE GREAT FIRE OF LONDON IN 1666. BY 1675, SIR CHRISTOPHER WREN HAD DESIGNED THE PRESENT CATHEDRAL, WITH ITS FAMOUS DOME, WHICH WAS COMPLETED IN ABOUT 1710.

Throughout history, many sovereigns, or leaders, have been crowned in Westminster Abbey. For the coronation of Queen Elizabeth II in 1953, more than 8,000 people crammed into the abbey for the first coronation to be televised live.

The Coronation Chair is placed in front of the High Altar in the **Sacrarium**. The new sovereign is **anointed** with holy oil, and puts on the coronation robes and **regalia**. Finally, St. Edward's Crown is placed on the sovereign's head. The service has not changed for hundreds of years.

ROYAL WEDDINGS

Westminster Abbey is also used for royal weddings and funerals. The last royal wedding in the abbey was that of Prince William and Kate Middleton in 2011.

Kate Middleton, Prince William, and Queen Elizabeth II appear with page boys and a bridesmaid on the balcony of Buckingham Palace after the royal wedding of 2011.

The funeral of Diana, Princess of Wales, in 1997 is believed to have been one of the most watched live television events in history.

Prince William's grandparents, the then Princess Elizabeth and Prince Philip, married in the abbey in 1947. William's aunt, Princess Anne, and his uncle, Prince Andrew, also married in the abbey. William's parents, Prince Charles and Princess Diana, were married at St. Paul's Cathedral.

FUNERALS AND TOMBS

Less happy royal occasions are funerals. In 1997, Princess Diana's funeral was held at the abbey. The princess's sudden death in a car accident was news around the world. Estimates suggest more than two billion people watched the funeral on TV. Princess Diana was not buried at the abbey, however, but in the grounds of her childhood home. Most of the kings and queens buried within the abbey date from the medieval period. In that way, the abbey represents a permanent memorial to the early centuries of English history.

TIMELINE

604 The first version of St. Paul's Cathedral is built in London.

c. 960 Bishop Dunstan sends monks to found an abbey on Thorney Island, west of St. Paul's.

1042 Around now, King Edward starts building a new abbey at the site.

1065 The new abbey is consecrated.

1066 King Edward dies and is buried in the abbey. After the conquest of England by Prince William of Normandy, he is crowned in the abbey as King William I, beginning the tradition of royal coronations in the abbey.

1090 Edward's church is finally completed.

1161 Edward is recognized as a saint and named "the Confessor." Two years later his tomb is moved close to the High Altar.

1245 King Henry III demolishes the old church for a new building in the Gothic style.

1269 Edward the Confessor is reburied near the new High Altar.

1272 King Henry III dies; he is buried inside the abbey. Work on the abbey comes to a halt.

1296 King Edward I captures the Stone of Scone in Scotland and brings it to Westminster Abbey.

1376 Work on the abbey restarts, following Henry III's original design.

1509 The main body of the new abbey is completed.

1516 The first Tudor monarch, King Henry VII, consecrates the Lady Chapel inside the abbey.

1530s King Henry VIII decides to break with the Roman Catholic Church and create his own Protestant Church of England. He begins to dissolve Catholic monasteries in England and Wales.

1540 Henry VIII dissolves Westminster Abbey and it is handed over to him.

1556 The poet Geoffrey Chaucer is buried in the abbey in recognition of his role as an official at the Palace of Westminster.

1560 Queen Elizabeth I refounds the abbey as a Protestant church under her direct control, a "royal peculiar."

1599 The poet Edmund Spenser is buried next to Chaucer, beginning the tradition of Poets' Corner.

1674 The remains of the bodies believed to be the Princes in the Tower are found at the Tower of London. They are later reburied in the abbey.

1920 The Unknown Warrior is buried in the abbey.

1941 The abbey is badly damaged by bombs during the Blitz.

1953 Queen Elizabeth II is crowned in the abbey.

1996 The Stone of Scone is removed from the Coronation Chair and returned to Scotland.

1997 More than two billion TV viewers around the world watch the funeral of Diana, Princess of Wales, held in the abbey.

2015 During building works, up to 50 skeletons from the 1000s and 1100s are discovered outside the abbey.

GLOSSARY

anointed Rubbed with oil as part of a ceremony.

apse A large semicircular section at the eastern end of a church.

battens Long, flat strips of wood used to hold something in place.

Benedictine Belonging to the order of monks founded by St. Benedict.

ceremonial Used in ceremonies and rituals.

clergy All the officials of the Christian church.

collegiate Describes a church that is not under the control of a bishop.

commemorate To celebrate the achievements of someone who has died.

consecrated Declared sacred.

Confessor A person who sticks to their faith in the face of hostility.

fan vaulting An arched ceiling held up by ribs spread in the shape of a fan.

Gothic A style of architecture popular from the 1100s to the 1500s, with pointed arches, ribbed vaults, and large windows.

High Altar The main altar of a church.

masons People who cut and shape stone.

memorial A statue or other object that reminds people of someone who has died.

minster A church or cathedral originally connected to a monastery.

missionary A person who tries to convert people to a religion.

monumental Serving as a monument or memorial.

nave The central part of a church where the congregation sits.

octagonal Having eight sides.

pagan A person whose religious beliefs are not those of the world's main religions.

parliament The group of people that make laws in a country.

plaque A tablet fixed to a wall to commemorate a person or an event.

predecessor The person who held an office before the current person.

regalia The symbols of royalty.

Remembrance Day A memorial day in the British Commonwealth for those who have died in war.

Romanesque A style of architecture used from the 500s to the 900s, with semicircular arches.

sacrarium The part of a church holding the high altar.

saints' days Days on which particular saints are celebrated in church.

shrine A holy place associated with a particular person.

tapestry A piece of fabric with designs woven into it.

transepts Arms of a church at right angles to the nave.

Tudor Related to the Tudor family, which ruled England from 1485 to 1603.

undercroft A cellar beneath a church, usually used for storage.

FURTHER INFORMATION

Books

Baum, Margaux, and David Hilliam
Castles and Cathedrals (Life in the Middle Ages). New York: Rosen Central, 2017.

Carmack, Amanda.
Murder at Westminster Abbey. (An Elizabethan Mystery). New York: Obsidian, 2014.

Goldsworthy, Kaite.
St. Paul's Cathedral (Houses of Faith). New York: AV2 by Weigl, 2014.

MacDonald, Fiona.
You Wouldn't Want to Work on a Medieval Cathedral.
New York: Franklin Watts, 2010.

Websites

www.westminster-abbey.org/our-history
A detailed history of the abbey with links to pages about its architecture and the people buried there.

www.ducksters.com/history/middle_ages/catholic_church_cathedrals.php
A guide to medieval cathedrals, how they were built, and what they meant to the people who built them.

www.historyforkids.net/edward-the-confessor.html
The story of Edward the Confessor, the monarch who was responsible for making Westminster Abbey so important.

Publisher's note to educators and parents: Our editors have carefully reviewed these websites to ensure that they are suitable for students. Many websites change frequently, however, and we cannot guarantee that a site's future contents will continue to meet our high standards of quality and educational value. Be advised that students should be closely supervised whenever they access the Internet.

INDEX